BETSY'S DAY at the GAME

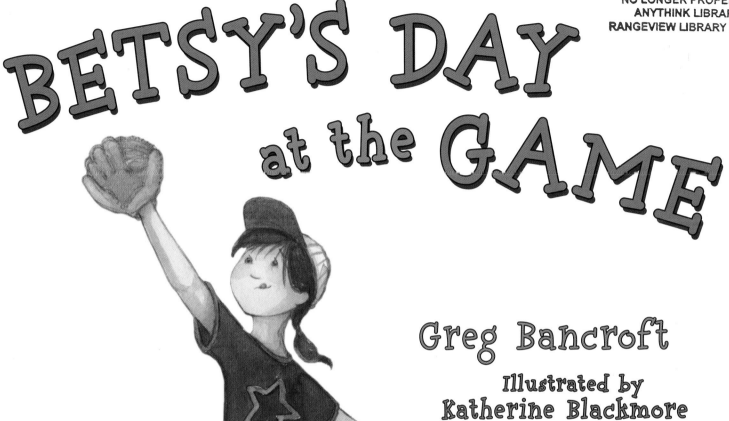

Greg Bancroft

Illustrated by
Katherine Blackmore

SCARLETTA KIDS

MINNEAPOLIS, MINNESOTA

Published by Scarletta Kids, an imprint of Scarletta

This book is a work of fiction. Names, characters, places, events, and incidents are either a product of the author's imagination or are used fictitiously. Any resemblance to reality is entirely coincidental.

The Lexile Framework for Reading® Lexile measure® 670L

Library of Congress Cataloging-in-Publication Data

Bancroft, Greg.
 Betsy's day at the game / by Greg Bancroft ; illustrated by Katherine Blackmore. -- 1st ed.
     p. cm.
 Summary: Betsy spends a wonderful and exciting day at the ball park with her beloved grandfather, demonstrating to him all she has learned about keeping score. Includes instructions and a scorecard.
 ISBN 978-1-938063-01-5 (pbk. : alk. paper) -- ISBN 1-938063-01-5 (pbk. : alk. paper) --
ISBN 978-1-938063-02-2 (electronic) -- ISBN 1-938063-02-3 (electronic)
[1. Baseball--Fiction. 2. Baseball--Scorekeeping--Fiction. 3. Grandfathers--Fiction.]
I. Blackmore, Katherine, ill. II. Title.
 PZ7.B2188Bet 2013
 [E]--dc23
                                    2012030410

Book Design by Kelly Doudna, Mighty Media Inc., Minneapolis, MN

Distributed by Publishers Group West

Printed and manufactured in the United States
North Mankato, MN

First edition
10 9 8 7 6 5 4 3 2 1

For everyone who's ever heard
the crack of the bat!

— Greg Bancroft

In loving and joyful memory
of my dad, Tom Mason.

— Katherine Blackmore

"Elisabeth, Grandpa's here," Betsy's mom called out. A car pulled in to the driveway. Betsy came running with her Boo Bag.

"Grandpa!" Betsy shrieked as she jumped into his arms. Her grandfather swung her around and gave her a kiss.

"Are you ready for some baseball, Betsy Boo?" he asked her, using her nickname.

"She's been ready since breakfast," her mother answered. "She's been making sure she had everything in her Boo Bag."

Betsy smiled. She had remembered her glove, score book, pencil, and hat. They were all in her special bag.

"Let's go," Grandpa said. They buckled up and drove to the ballpark.

Along the way, the two of them talked about all the things that had happened at Betsy's house the past week. Betsy and her brother, Peter, each skinned a knee, the new kitten, Noodles, climbed high in the tree and was rescued by some linemen working nearby, she stayed at her best friend Kelly's house and watched scary movies, Uncle Joe cooked something really good, and she read two new books.

"Wow," Grandpa said, chuckling a bit. "That's quite a list. Noodles in the tree would have been a big week all by itself."

"No kidding," Betsy agreed. "All that—and baseball too!"

"It doesn't get much better," they said in unison and nodded to each other.

Betsy put on her cap.

Soon, they were at the ballpark. On the outside, it was a tall building with walkways everywhere. Flags fluttered on their poles. There were people and noise all around. They were in the middle of a very busy part of the city. The ballpark added to the commotion. Betsy walked close to Grandpa and held his hand tightly. Her Boo Bag was slung over her shoulder. She wasn't scared, just overwhelmed. There were vendors and souvenirs, loud music, smoky grills, and legs.

7

Legs everywhere.
It was difficult to
see very far ahead,
but it was very exciting.
She couldn't wait to get
inside the park.

In the middle of the
crowded city, the brick
walls opened up to reveal a
beautiful baseball diamond.
Like a pop-up book. It was
magic. They had great seats.
Betsy could see every part of
the field perfectly.

She turned to Grandpa
and asked, "What do you

like the most—smelling the grass, reading the scoreboard, or watching the people?"

He took a deep breath. "I like the smell of the grass."

Betsy took a deep breath. "Me too."

"Actually," Grandpa said as he leaned into her, kissing the top of her head, "I like it all … and I especially like it when I'm with you, Boo!"

Betsy was so happy. She wanted this day to last forever. Then she remembered! Her score book! It was nearly game time, and she had not written anything in it yet. She quickly retrieved it from her Boo Bag, along with her pencil, and began to write. In the margin, she wrote about Noodles, the skinned knees, the scary movies, and Uncle Joe. She noted that it had been a very hot and humid week.

"Got everything in there?" Grandpa asked. He remembered when another little girl used to do the same thing in her score book.

"I can't wait to show it to Mom," Betsy said.

"Yes, your mom told me that you have been practicing how to keep score," Grandpa said.

"That's right," Betsy said with delight. "May I show you what I've learned so far?"

"I'd love that," Grandpa said gladly.

"Well, the first thing you have to know is that each player has a number," Betsy said in a big-girl voice.

"I know," Grandpa teased. "I can see a number on everyone's shirt." Betsy laughed. "No, silly, each player has a number that means the same thing as the position that he plays."

"Give me an example," Grandpa said. He was just testing her. He had been keeping score at baseball games since he was Betsy's age.

"Okay. You look at each person, tell me the position they are playing, and I will tell you the number that I'll use in my score book."

"Pitcher," Grandpa started off.

"One," Betsy replied confidently.

"Catcher," Grandpa continued.

"Two," Betsy said.

"First base," Grandpa said.

"Three," Betsy followed.

"Second base."

"Four."

"Now here is where things get tricky," Grandpa cautioned.

"I know what you're thinking. You could try to trick me by saying 'shortstop'—the guy next to the second baseman," Betsy warned Grandpa, pretending to sound stern. "But let's go to the third baseman. He's number five."

"Then what number is the shortstop?" Grandpa pretended not to know.

"Six."

"Ah," he said, nodding his head like he was hearing the news for the first time.

"Now, the outfield is pretty simple," Betsy said boldly. "Left, center, right. Seven, eight, nine."

She and Grandpa then filled in the names of the players for each team. They also listed each player's

SCOREKEEPING CODES

Each position has a number
1 = pitcher
2 = catcher
3 = first baseman
4 = second baseman
5 = third baseman
6 = shortstop
7 = left fielder
8 = center fielder
9 = right fielder

jersey number and position number. They opened up the score book all the way to admire their handiwork.

"I get it," Grandpa replied. "It's a lot easier to put one simple number in your score book instead of trying to write out the person's position all the time!"

"Grandpa, you're so smart," Betsy said fondly as she patted his hand. He seemed to be blinking hard as he smiled, holding back a tear. But he does that a lot, she reminded herself: at family gatherings, when he tells stories about being in the Navy, and at baseball games. And sure enough, he seemed to be blinking hard as they sat back down after singing the National Anthem.

The home team ran onto the field. "There's Happy, Grandpa, look!" Betsy yelled and pointed to her favorite player.

"I see, I see," Grandpa said excitedly. He liked their team's star shortstop, Jorge Rodriguez. He was fast, a great hitter, and caught nearly every ball hit his way. He was also known for his great sense of humor and Hollywood smile. His nickname really suited him well. He was very happy and made others around him happy, including the fans.

"Grandpa," Betsy said, pointing to her score book, "don't you just love the way this looks?"

"I do, indeed," he said. "Each one of those little squares is for one at bat. There is a picture of a

Jorge Rodriguez

baseball diamond, tiny boxes to keep track of balls and strikes, and little letters to mark how the batter got on base. Tidy. Neat."

"And no two games will ever be exactly alike," Betsy added.

"It doesn't get much better," they said again in unison and nodded to each other.

Betsy and Grandpa munched on hot dogs and drank sodas while the pitcher threw a few warm-up tosses to the catcher. Then the umpire swept home plate with his little broom and yelled, "Play ball!"

"Do you have your glove ready?" Grandpa asked.

16

Betsy reached into her Boo Bag and got her glove out—just in case a ball came her way that she might catch.

The visiting team's first batter was Jacob Smith. He stepped into the batter's box. He wiggled his feet into the dirt, tapped the bat on the plate, and stared at the pitcher, Tyler White. It was time to play ball—and keep score!

"Steeee….rrrrrrrr…..iiiiiii……kkkkkk…… eeeee!" the umpire yelled, as the first pitch came screaming in at 95 miles per hour. Betsy marked one of the tiny boxes for a strike. The next pitch was also a strike. Betsy marked a box for it, too. Smith swung at the third pitch and missed. He trotted to the dugout and sat down on the bench, apparently not too happy with himself. Betsy put

Jacob Smith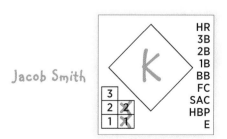

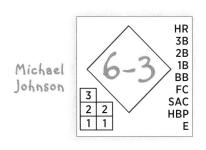

Michael Johnson

6-3

HR
3B
2B
1B
BB
FC
SAC
HBP
E

a big "K" on the picture of the diamond for his at bat. That shows that the batter struck out. One down.

Michael Johnson was up second. He hit the first pitch hard on the ground to Happy. Happy scooped it up easily and threw it hard to David Moore at first base. Betsy put "6-3" on the picture of the diamond. That shows that the batter hit a ball to the shortstop who threw it to first base before the batter got to the bag. Two down.

Josh Williams was up third. He hit two pitches off to the side. They were foul balls. Betsy knew that the first two fouls counted as strikes. She made marks for two strikes. Then the pitcher threw three more pitches that were out of the strike zone. The umpire called them all balls.

"White better watch out," Betsy warned Grandpa. "The count is three balls and two strikes."

"Yep," Grandpa said. "A full count. He just needs one more strike, and it will be the third out. Now he might walk this guy."

"One more ball and—" Betsy was interrupted. The umpire called the next pitch a ball, and the batter trotted down to first base. Betsy circled the little "BB" printed in the little square. That shows that the batter walked, or got a "base on balls." She drew a line from home plate to first base. That shows that there is now a runner at first base. He could possibly run around all the bases and eventually score.

Josh Williams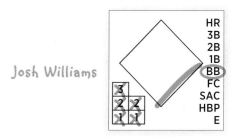

"Uh-oh," Betsy said, shaking her head. "You sure don't want to be letting people on base for free."

"No you don't," her grandfather agreed. "Especially when The Crusher is the next batter." Grandpa was referring to Matt Brown, the fourth man in the lineup. The Crusher was a huge, muscular man known for smacking baseballs far into the home run stands.

The Crusher swung so hard at the first pitch that he spun around in the batter's box and almost fell over when he missed the ball. Betsy chuckled as she made a mark for strike one. What happened next was almost too good to be true.

The Crusher hit the very next pitch high in the sky, but way back. Back toward the seats that Betsy and Grandpa were in. She quickly put

on her glove. It came right to her! She stuck out her glove and caught it!

"Grandpa!" she yelled, holding up the ball, "I caught it!"

"You sure did! Way to go!" Grandpa exclaimed as he patted her on the back.

Everyone was cheering for her. Someone pointed out the instant replay on the big screen. Everyone cheered again as they saw the little girl with her tongue sticking out catch the foul ball hit by The Crusher. Betsy smiled, but she was embarrassed.

"What's wrong, my darling Boo?" Grandpa wondered.

"Whenever I concentrate really hard, my tongue sticks out a little bit," Betsy said sheepishly. "It makes me look silly." Grandpa hugged her close, the way grandpas do when they don't have words to help little girls feel better.

Just then, the crowd starting cheering again. The Crusher had hit a ball high and deep to center field. Betsy and her grandfather watched the replay. They watched as Joe Anderson leaped high into the air and caught the ball. The ball had already gone past the top of the fence, but the center fielder reached way over, crashed into the fence, and grabbed the ball in his mitt.

"Wow!" Betsy shouted above the noise. "Grandpa, did you see that catch?"

"I sure did," Grandpa replied. "Anderson robbed The Crusher of a home run!"

Betsy put "F-8" on the picture of the diamond for The Crusher's at bat. That shows that the batter

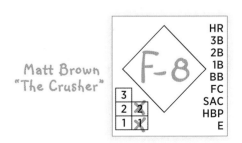

hit a fly ball that was caught by the center fielder. Third out. She would just have to tell people what a great catch it was.

Innings came and went. Both teams had chances to score runs. But neither team did. The score remained zero to zero until the ninth inning. The visiting team got a lot of hits in the top of the inning. Three players ran around all the bases and touched home plate. The home team finally got the third out. But the score was zero to three. Betsy's team was losing.

Betsy opened up her score book all the way. There were dark diamonds in the squares for the three opposing players who had scored runs. She had filled them in with her pencil, careful to stay within the lines. All the little pictures of diamonds on her team's side only had a few dark lines, none were filled in completely.

"Oh, Grandpa," Betsy sounded worried. "We're losing. We're only up one more time." That meant her team had only one more chance to try to score runs. Three more outs, and the game would be over.

"I know, my darling Boo," Grandpa said. "But it's not over until it's over."

It was the bottom of the ninth inning. Alex Martin was up first. He walked. Four pitches out of the strike zone meant that he got a base on balls. When it's your team, Betsy thought, it's good when a player gets on base for free.

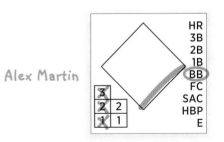

Nick Jackson hit two long foul balls. Betsy hoped that two other kids got to go home with those baseballs. She smiled as she saw hers safe in her Boo Bag.

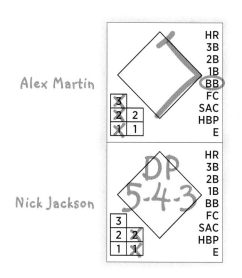

Alex Martin

Nick Jackson

On the third pitch, Jackson hit a hard ground ball to the third baseman that looked like it might shoot into left field. Somehow, Johnson grabbed it and threw it to Diego Garcia at second base. Garcia stepped on the bag, jumped over the sliding Alex Martin, and threw the ball to Danny Jones at first. It was a 5-4-3 double play. Martin and Jackson were both out.

"Oh, Grandpa," Betsy moaned.

"I know, I know," Grandpa tried to sound reassuring.

"We only have one more out," Betsy sounded worried. "We need three runs to tie the game, four to win it."

"It's not over until it's over," Grandpa reminded her.

"You're right," Betsy sighed.

Betsy put on her "rally cap." She turned her hat inside out and put it on her head backwards. It was a silly tradition that people did, hoping that it might bring their team good luck. Right then, her team needed all the help it could get.

The next batter was Ryan Thompson. He hit a ball to right field that the fielder couldn't catch. A solid single. Betsy circled the little "1B" for his at bat and drew a dark line from home to first.

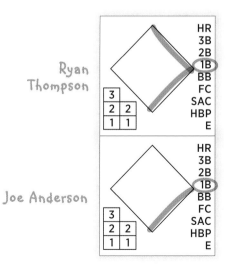

Joe Anderson was up next and singled too, only to left field. She made the same marks for him. Then she went to Thompson's square and drew a line from first base to second base.

27

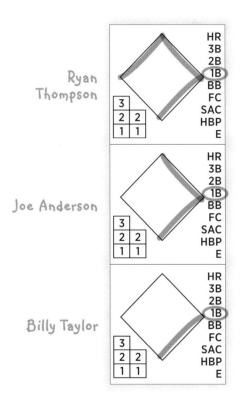

Ryan Thompson

Joe Anderson

Billy Taylor

Then Billy Taylor got a hit, too! There were runners marked in three separate squares in Betsy's score book. Thompson was now at third base. Anderson was now at second base. And Taylor was at first base. The bases were loaded! The crowd was standing and cheering. Everyone was so excited.

"Haaaaa.....pppppp.....yyyyyyy!" the crowd yelled. Everybody's favorite player was coming up to bat. Happy Rodriguez was wiggling his feet into the dirt in the batter's box. The bases were loaded. There were two outs. He needed to get a hit so at least one of the runners could score. A home run would score everyone and win the game!

"Oh, Grandpa!" Betsy shouted above the cheers. He smiled and looked at her.

"It doesn't get much better," they said in unison and nodded to each other.

Happy swung at two pitches and missed. Then the pitcher threw the next three balls out of the strike zone. Full count. The crowd was so loud, Betsy had to concentrate really hard. She didn't even care if people saw her tongue sticking out. The next pitch could decide the game.

Crack!

Time stood still. The crowd was almost silent. Everyone watched as the baseball flew high and deep, out toward left field. Happy let the bat slip from his hands and started running to first. The men on base were running too. When the ball hit the stairs of the upper deck in left field, everyone

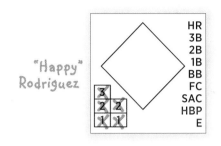

"Happy" Rodriguez

HR
3B
2B
1B
BB
FC
SAC
HBP
E

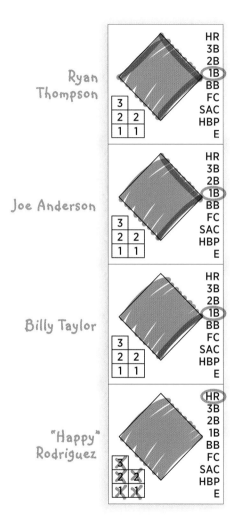

Ryan Thompson

Joe Anderson

Billy Taylor

"Happy" Rodriguez

started jumping up and down. Except for the visiting team. They were still.

The runners all touched home plate. Happy trotted around all the bases and jumped on home plate. Then his whole team jumped on him. He had just hit a grand slam home run to win the game! The final score was four to three. The best part was when Betsy watched the replay on the scoreboard. When it showed Happy hitting the ball, she was convinced that she could see his tongue sticking out a little bit.

"Grandpa," Betsy said, hugging him as hard as she could, "this was the best day ever! Thank you so much for taking me to the game!"

"You are very welcome, Betsy Boo," Grandpa

replied as he hugged her tightly. "Let's get home to tell your mom what a great day this was."

"It doesn't get much better," they said in unison and nodded to each other.

Betsy put her glove, her score book, and her pencil back into her Boo Bag. She turned her hat right-side out again and put it back on her head. She swung her Boo Bag over her shoulder. She held her ball in one hand and grabbed Grandpa's hand with the other as they made their way back to the car. She was very tired, but very happy.

Her mother had listened to the game on the radio as she worked in the garden. She knew the score and that Happy had hit a grand slam home run. All through dinner, Betsy talked and talked about her day at the game. She talked and talked some more about what a great day it was as she took a bath and got ready for bed.

Her mom was excited that Betsy had caught a ball, and from The Crusher himself! She patted Betsy's hand as she heard about her tongue sticking out on the big screen. She was patient as Betsy reviewed her score book and told her about the great catch that Anderson had made in center field. She smiled as she saw the notes from the week that Betsy had written on the pages.

"Now I want to show you something," her mom said as Betsy was climbing into bed. "Take a look."

She gave Betsy a very worn and slightly yellowed score book.

"Your grandpa gave me this when I was about your age," her mom said fondly. "Look inside."

Betsy opened it up. She saw lots of little marks that told the stories of the games. She could imagine balls and strikes, hits that batters made, and runs scored. She also saw notes about what had been happening in her mom's life during those weeks when she kept score at baseball games. She also saw one game where her mother made a note about catching a ball.

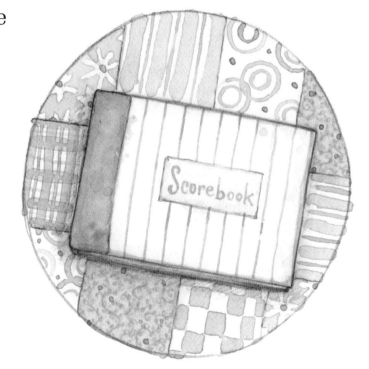

"Mom, I never knew you caught a ball!" Betsy exclaimed.

"Here it is." Her mom held out a baseball with a date written on it and the score of the game.

"We lost that day," she lamented, "but it was still one of the greatest days ever."

"Why?" asked Betsy.

"Because I was with your grandpa," she replied, "and it was fun to be at the game with him, keeping score, laughing, eating hot dogs, and holding his hand." She squeezed her eyes tightly as she smiled.

"Just like Grandpa," Betsy said as she squeezed her eyes tightly and smiled.

"It doesn't get much better," they said in unison and nodded to each other.

THE END

HOW TO KEEP SCORE

- List the players in the order they will bat. Use a separate page for each team's batting order.

- Write down the names of the players in the "PLAYER" column. The "NO." column is for the players' numbers. The "POS." column is for the players' fielding positions.

- Each player has a row of squares next to his name. That's where you record what happens during each at bat. There is a column for each inning.

- If a batter gets on base, circle the code for how he did it. Trace the lines on the diamond to the base where he ended up.

EXAMPLES

single

double

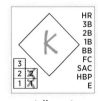

walk

- If a batter makes an out, mark it in the middle of the diamond. Use the code for the type of out he made. Add the number for any fielder who was part of the play.

EXAMPLES

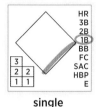

fly to left fielder

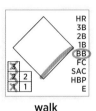

ground ball to third baseman who threw it to first baseman

strikeout

- If a runner already on base advances or gets out, be sure to mark that too.

- If a runner scores, fill in the whole diamond. That makes the runs easy to count.

- After the third out in an inning, draw a line below the last batter's square. That helps you remember to use the next column for the next inning.

SCOREKEEPING CODES

Each position has a number or letters

1 = pitcher
2 = catcher
3 = first baseman
4 = second baseman
5 = third baseman
6 = shortstop
7 = left fielder
8 = center fielder
9 = right fielder
DH = designated hitter

CODES FOR GETTING ON BASE AND ADVANCING

HR = home run
3B = triple
2B = double
1B = single
BB = walk
IBB = intentional walk
FC = fielder's choice
HBP = hit by pitch
E = error
I = interference
WP = wild pitch
PB = passed ball
BK = balk

CODES FOR OUTS

K = swinging strikeout
Ʞ = called strikeout
F = fly out
L = line out
U = unassisted out
DP = double play
SAC = sacrifice
CS = caught stealing
PO = pick-off

NO.	PLAYER	POS.	1	2	3	4	5	6	7	8	9	10		NOTES

TEAM NAME: **GAME DATE / TIME:** **BALLPARK:**

Each batter cell contains a diamond with the markings: HR, 3B, 2B, 1B, BB, FC, SAC, HBP, E and count boxes 3 / 2 2 / 1 1.

Right-hand column for each player: AB____ R____ H____ RBI____

| | | TOTALS | R/H | | | | | | | | | | | | |

PITCHERS		IP	H	R	ER	BB	SO	WP	W/L	DOUBLE PLAYS:
										2BH:
										3BH:
										HR:
										PASSED BALLS:

NO.	PLAYER	POS.	1	2	3	4	5	6	7	8	9	10		NOTES

Each batter cell contains: HR, 3B, 2B, 1B, BB, FC, SAC, HBP, E with baseball diamond and count boxes (3, 2, 2, 1, 1).

Right column per row: AB, R, H, RBI

TOTALS   R/H

PITCHERS	IP	H	R	ER	BB	SO	WP	W/L	DOUBLE PLAYS:
									2BH:
									3BH:
									HR:
									PASSED BALLS:

SCORECARD EXAMPLE FILLED OUT

INNING 6

1. Smith walks.
2. Johnson singles. Smith goes to second base.
3. Williams hit into a double play, shortstop to second base to first base. Johnson is out at second. Smith goes to third base.
4. Brown called out on strikes.

INNING 7

1. Jones lines out to third base.
2. Miller doubles.
3. Davis grounds out, second base to first base. Miller goes to third base.
4. Garcia triples. Miller scores.
5. Wilson flies out to right field.

NO.	PLAYER	POS.	6	7
1	Jacob Smith	7		
25	Michael Johnson	5		
13	Josh Williams	6	DP 6-4-3	
28	Matt Brown "The Crusher"	DH	K	
14	Danny Jones	3		L5
26	Chris Miller	9		
19	Andrew Davis	8		4-3
12	Diego Garcia	4		
3	Ethan Wilson	2		F-9
	TOTALS	R/H	0 / 1	1 / 2
	PITCHERS		SO	WP
29	Luis Martinez	1		

TEAM NAME:

Gregory Bancroft, an avid baseball fan, shares an experience of going to a game that mirrors his own time spent with his kids. Growing up, Greg loved being outdoors, especially playing baseball in the summers. He holds degrees from the University of Minnesota, Yale, and Luther Seminary. He and his wife live in Minneapolis near Lake Nokomis, while his children and grandchildren are scattered across the country.

Katherine Blackmore, has a BFA in illustration from the Cleveland Institute of Art, and has been a professional artist for 20 years, during which she worked at the Walt Disney Feature Animation Studio. Her screen credits include: *The Hunchback of Notre Dame*, *Mulan*, *Tarzan*, *Lilo & Stitch*, and *Brother Bear*. She currently teaches 2-D animation at a university in Orlando, Florida. Katherine has numerous hobbies and especially enjoys reading, gardening, traveling, yoga, and hang gliding. She resides in Edgewood, Florida, with her husband and their three cats.